Hotwife Vacation - A M F M Multiple Partner Wife Watching Wife Sharing Romance Novel

Karly Violet

Published by Karly Violet, 2021.

HOTWIFE VACATION - A M F M MULTIPLE PARTNER WIFE WATCHING WIFE SHARING ROMANCE NOVEL

First edition. December 6, 2021.

Copyright © 2021 Karly Violet.

ISBN: 979-8201419127

Written by Karly Violet.

Hotel Vacation

A M F M Multiple Partner Wife Watching Wife Sharing Romance Novel

Chapter One: Long Days, Short Nights

"How's things going in here?" I ask as I walk into my wife's office.

Renee looks up at me from her desk and frowns. "Is it just me, or are the days getting longer and longer?" Her blue eyes turn to the cup of coffee in my hand. "And where's mine, Dom?"

I chuckle. "You didn't ask me to make you a cup, my love. Would you like some coffee?"

"Of course I do." She raises an eyebrow and laughs as I turn and walk back into my office across the small hallway. As I pour a cup of coffee for her, I think about the weeks we have spent in here working hard to get our new law firm up and running. Things have been hectic and at times a little disheartening, but it seems that we're about to have everything working the way that it should.

"Here you go," I say as I put the cup of hot coffee down on her desk top. Renee smiles before taking a drink. "Do you still have the McLaughlin account here?"

My wife looks up and nods her head. "I should have given this fucking file to you to begin with, Dom. It's full of all sorts of mistakes. What the hell did their previous attorney do for three hundred per hour?"

I shrug my shoulders. "I don't know. What's funny is how hard the managers there fought to keep that same guy on retainer. They've had three lawsuits in the last year and settled all of them out of court. Honestly, they shouldn't have settled any of them."

"Eh, maybe the first one," Renee replies as she looks at her computer. "The employee that slipped on the wet floor and tore her rotator cuff had a pretty solid case. The other two, though, I have to agree. They got themselves ripped open financially because of a second-rate attorney that was way overpriced."

I love to watch my wife work in her office. She's likely one of the best attorneys in the business and it's why we've decided to open our practice together after being beholden to other people and law firms for so long. I've spent six years of my legal career working for corporate America, and it has drained me terribly. To be my own boss and to share the work with my beautiful wife is a dream come true. An expensive one, but a good one nonetheless.

"We need a break from this," I say to her. "A way to recharge our batteries before things get even busier this fall."

"A break. Yeah, that would be nice," my petite wife says with a smile as her blonde ponytail sways from side to side. "A vacation somewhere would be even better."

"Oh. Like a trip?"

"Yeah, not some visit to the mountains to hike or anything like that. Maybe we could go to the Virgin Islands or the Bahamas."

I nod my head. "We really do deserve something special, huh?" My mind is full of images of Renee in a two-piece bikini. She's a sexy woman, only five-two and weighing barely a hundred pounds. A spinner by any definition, my wife can do all sorts of things in the bedroom if she has a mind to. That's been an issue lately, though. Actually, it's been a problem our entire eight years of marriage. She loves sex, which is great, but she isn't very adventurous in the bedroom. Some things are just off-limits no matter what.

"When, though?"

"I'll check the calendar." I pull my cell phone out of my pocket and open up our work calendar. My wife and I have been covered up for a while with the work we are doing for our new clients, which is a good thing. It means plenty of money coming into our new firm. "Early next month we have a week with nothing scheduled so far," I tell her. "What if we took that week off and went somewhere?"

Renee smiles. "I would love that, Dom. So, where could we go?"

"Like you said, to the Virgin Islands or the Bahamas. Any preference?"

My wife nods her head. "I want to go to Nassau if there's something available there. I've never been there and I'm told it's absolutely beautiful."

"I've heard that too." I smile at my beautiful mate. How badly I want to make her happy and to spend time with her on the beach in the Bahamas. Nassau would be a great location. "Let me look on my computer and see what I can find." I turn and go back to my office where I have a seat behind my desk. As I begin to look on travel websites, I notice that things are filling up very quickly. If we're going to find a place to stay in Nassau, I have to act fast. So, I book one of the more expensive hotels on the island and swallow hard as I look at the price tag. Using my American Express card, I book the room as well as a flight to the island before I hop up from my chair to inform Renee of the plans.

"Well, I got us a room and airline tickets," I say as I smile sheepishly at my wife.

She looks up from her work. "And? I get the feeling there's an *and* here, Dom." Renee is always quick to read another person's facial expressions. She's known me long enough that I'm like an open book to her.

"And it's not cheap," I reply. "Still, I booked the entire trip. It's all set." She sighs. "How much?"

"You don't want to know," I say to her. "Don't ask and I'll be sure to pay it off over the next few months, alright? Like you said, we deserve this trip, honey. You and I are long overdue for some time to ourselves and this is a great opportunity."

"Oh, Dominique." Whenever Renee is upset or worried about something, she uses my entire first name. Though she knew that a trip to the Bahamas on such short notice would likely not be cheap, I'm sure my wife also didn't want to break the bank. We haven't, yet. That will come as I try to pay for the trip in about six monthly installments on the American Express card.

"We can probably write it off for business, you know? I'll look at what we can do while there to do that."

"Uh, no. You know better than that, Dom. Don't screw with our taxes like that. The last thing we need is to have the IRS breathing down our necks."

"Honey, you worry too much," I say with a chuckle. "You do remember that I worked for a large company at one time and that's what I did with most of my time; find loopholes?"

"Loopholes in contracts and agreements with their vendors, not tax law. I'm just as confident in your legal abilities as you are, but you're not a tax attorney. We'll take this vacation as a personal trip and not worry about finding a way to write it off. Remember, the IRS doesn't hold back when they go after attorneys. They'll hammer us hard if they think we're screwing with the paperwork." Renee is right. At least, as far as how the IRS will respond to an attorney doing something they think is shady. Even so, I know that there are ways to write the trip off on our taxes. A meeting or two with other attorneys on the islands and maybe some talk about working together will give us all the cover we need to get a tax break out of our vacation. Plenty of other people do this as well. Why not us?

"Anyway, we'll leave on the seventh and return on the sixteenth. How does that sound?"

"Did you put it on the calendar?" Renee asks with a slight smile. "You know that if it's not on the calendar, it doesn't exist, right?" We have joked about this very thing many times over.

"I'll get it on there right now. Just be ready to wear that little green bikini you bought last spring when we go to the beach. I want to see you strut your stuff." My cock hardens a little as I wink at my wife.

"You're terrible, Dom." She laughs as she blushes. I nod my head and turn to go back to my office and to the work that I still have to do. If I had the option, I would fuck Renee right now, but as it is we are at work and doing that just wouldn't be very professional. Not one bit.

My cell phone buzzes. It's a text message from one of our clients, Mr. Richardson. "Hey, I might need to sit down and discuss adding another client to your list. We have a vendor that works with us and their CEO is needing a corporate attorney for some work that could last six months to a year. Interested?"

"Absolutely," I text back.

"Great. When would be a good time?" I open up the calendar again. Remembering that we will be gone from the seventh until the sixteenth, I reply, "How about this afternoon? Will that work?"

"That's quick," he answers.

"I know, but we don't have any time available sooner. I'll come to you and the vendor." My cock is still hard from thinking about Renee in her bikini. I can't wait to see her on the sand in her outfit.

"Sounds good. I'll arrange it." This is the last text message I receive from Mr. Richardson, so I settle in to work on a contract another client needs by tomorrow. Things are looking to be very busy for us up until the trip to Nassau. However, when it comes time to be on vacation, we'll be on vacation. It's a needed trip and one that I am happy to take with my beautiful wife.

Chapter Two: Plenty of Hangups

It's a week until our trip to the Bahamas and we are both working to get things together for the trip. "And what about sunscreen?" Renee asks. "Shouldn't we take that?"

I shake my head. "You know how airport security can be, honey. They won't allow that giant bottle through security. All they let you have are the tiny bottles."

"Well, I don't have any smaller bottles of it," she replies with a bit of disgust. "What are we going to do?

Smiling at my wife from across the bedroom, I tell her, "We'll buy some when we get there. That's what most people do when they go for a vacation, baby. It's not a big deal." Renee is a consummate planner. The only reason we have been able to get the new law office going is because of her ability to list the things we needed to do and then put them in the best order going forward. I'm more of a wait and see what happens sort of guy. That drives my wife nuts sometimes, but I think it also helps to put a little spice into our marriage.

"And the body wash for you. My shampoo. They won't allow those either, will they?" Her blue eyes stare intensely into mine as if I have anything to do with what the TSA will or will not allow on airplanes.

"We'll have to get some when we arrive, Renee. It's fine, really. These are small things."

"But my shampoo is special, Dom. My hairstylist says it's the best one to keep my hair color from turning orange. You don't want me to have orange hair, do you?" Though Renee is serious about her shampoo, I can't help but smile. I love her because she can be a little neurotic sometimes.

"We'll find some good shampoo there, honey. You're not the first blonde woman to visit Nassau, after all. They'll have everything we need on the island." I sit down on our bed and watch my wife walking back and forth from the closet to one of her bags for just a moment. "I want us to try some things while we're there, too."

Renee stops for a moment and looks at me. "Try some things?"

I nod my head. "Sure. I want us to try a few things that we don't normally try. You know, just to expand our horizons while we're in the Bahamas."

My wife raises an eyebrow. "Like what new things? Fishing? Diving?"

I swallow hard before replying, "I mean sexually. I want us to try new things that maybe we don't do in the bedroom usually."

"Sexually?" She shakes her head. "We have sex, Dominique. We had sex just last night, remember?"

My heart beats hard as I try to frame my words carefully with my wife. "I mean I want us to try some sexual stuff that we don't do. Like anal."

"*Anal?*" Renee's eyes harden into a glare as she looks at me. "I don't like anal, Dom. You know that."

"I know you don't," I answer before adding, "But I want you to let me try anal with you again. I think we could both end up liking it a lot." Sex is something that Renee and I have discussed at length before. We have somewhat different ideas of what constitutes a healthy sexual lifestyle and that has sometimes caused us to butt heads over our bedroom time together. Though I don't want to start an argument with her just before heading out on a trip, I want to broach the idea of her becoming less prudish at least while we're on vacation.

"Dominique, I don't want you to put your dick inside my ass. It's painful and honestly, a little offensive too." She turns to go back to her closet to look at her beach outfits.

I sigh. "I know you don't like the idea of it, but I'm just asking that you keep an open mind about it. There are lots of married couples who do it and love it, baby."

"Love it?" Renee steps out of her closet. "Dom, I've talked to other women who have had anal sex with their husbands or boyfriends, and most of them have told me that they only do it because their significant others beg them to do it. They don't really like it." She shakes her head. "Besides, I have a pussy like any other woman. Isn't that enough for you?"

"And a mouth," I quickly add.

"Yeah a mouth. And I guess you want to complain about that part of me too, huh?"

"I'm not complaining," I reply as I realize just how stupid it was for me to bring up oral sex. "Not at all."

"Yes, you are." Renee walks up to me and stares into my eyes. "You don't like my blow jobs either. You've said as much to me before."

"No I haven't, honey. Don't put words in my mouth."

"Just put a dick into mine, huh?" My wife clenches her jaw as she shakes her head. "I suck on you whenever you want me to. You don't go without blow jobs, Dominique."

Feeling a little overwhelmed with the whole conversation, I retort, "You suck on it, yeah, but you never *finish* me off that way. You also don't swallow it, Renee. Why don't you at least try to swallow for me?"

She steps back, her facial expression changing as if I have just slapped her with a wet hand. "It gags me. The taste and texture of your semen are not great, Dom. You should try it sometime."

"That's what I'll do. I'll go find another dude and blow him so that I can swallow for him. Maybe that's what I have to do to experience a completed blow job one way or the other."

Renee's face turns red. "I give and give to you in that bed," she exclaims while pointing at our bed. "You get off, don't you? Since when have you not gotten off with me?"

"Hand jobs. Straight missionary sex. Sure, I get off, but only barely so sometimes. I have asked you to swallow and I've asked you for anal, but you always refuse to do either one. It's like you don't really care enough about me to finish me off in one of those ways, Renee. I don't mean to be an asshole, but there are a lot of women out there who service their husbands this way."

My wife huffs before going to her knees. "Fine. I'll show you." She pulls at my shorts, causing them to fall to my feet. Then my wife pulls my cock out of my briefs and shoves it into her mouth. My body bucks a little as I feel her mouth around my shaft.

"Wow," I chuckle as Renee begins to suck hard on me. "I didn't mean that you had to do that right now."

She pulls back just long enough to reply, "Just shut up, Dom." Renee pushes my pole back into her mouth and I enjoy the way she moves along my shaft, her tongue raking the underside of it. I love whenever my wife does this so unexpectedly. It's seldom in her nature to be spontaneous about anything sexual.

"Oh, shit," I say as I feel myself getting closer. Her blonde head bobs along my pecker as I put my hand on her head. My balls ache as I imagine Renee finally swallowing my thick man gravy. Maybe this will be the time that she finally does it? I can only hope so.

"*Ack...uttt...*" My wife pushes my cock to the back of her throat as I get closer to coming. "*Uttt...uttt...ack...*"

"Keep going," I plead with her as I put my other hand on her head. "I'm about there, honey. Show me that you can swallow. Fuck, I'm about there. *FUCK!!!*" I spurt hard and suddenly Renee pulls her head back, causing my second and third spurts to graze her cheek and land on her chest.

"*UTTTT!!! URP!!!*" She almost vomits as she holds my cock with her hand and turns to spit my jism onto the floor beside her.

"*Dammit! DAMMIT!!!*" I spurt a few more times before I pull away from her and walk to the bathroom. "Fuck."

"I tried," I hear her say from the bedroom. "You saw that I tried, Dom." Renee coughs a couple of times as she goes to the small trash can beside our bed and spits again. She can't stand any part of my spunk to be inside her mouth.

"Yeah, I know," I say with disappointment. "It's fine," I tell her. "Don't worry about it."

Renee comes into the bathroom and washes off her face as I finish wiping off my cock. Some of my own ball juice is on my legs and I'm forced to clean those as well.

"I tried," she says again. "Some women won't try at all, but I did."

"Yeah, okay." I walk out of the bathroom to where my jizz-covered shorts are lying on the floor. After putting them in the clothes hamper, I make my way to a drawer to find another pair. Shaking my head, I think about how difficult it has been to get Renee to do much more than just lie back and let me fuck her. I want more things added to our bedroom repertoire, but she just doesn't seem to be as interested in this as I am.

"I hate the texture," she argues as she stands on the other side of the bed. "You have to understand, it's not a natural texture. It's like yogurt."

I turn to look at her. "But you love yogurt. I don't see you gagging on that when you eat it, Renee."

Her eyes narrow as she shakes her head. "Your semen doesn't taste like yogurt. It tastes like some kind of earthy farm vegetable, Dominique. It's not exactly a satisfying flavor."

"Then it's flavor and not texture. Fine. Then we can use some fruity lube on my cock and then you can swallow, right? I mean, we can fix the flavor."

Renee scrunches her nose. "But it's still semen."

"And there it is," I reply. "It's the *thought* of what it is more than anything else. You don't want to swallow *semen*. Lucky me." I realize this is a sort of verbal cheap shot at my wife, but there's a lot of truth in it. Renee has never liked to have my jism in her mouth. She's always spit it out, though she did manage to accidentally swallow it one time when we were dating. That convinced me at the time that she could actually deliver quality oral sex. Had I known that she couldn't earlier on, it might have changed my thoughts on marrying her. Though sad, it's true. Sex does have something to do with the marital agreement, doesn't it?

"You're being vulgar and rude, Dominique. You should apologize to me right now."

"For what?" I quickly answer. "I eat you out all the time, Renee. You love it, too."

"But I don't *ejaculate* into your mouth."

"But you do get wet and I end up eating that," I tell my wife. "Renee, I am willing to do whatever you want to make you happy in bed. I've told you that many, many times before. You've asked for things, both orally and otherwise, and I've come through for you, right? Unfortunately, when it comes to you doing the same for me, you either can't do it or you won't. It's a little ego-crushing for a guy when his own wife won't swallow his cum."

"I can't fucking stand it!" Renee's eyes fill with tears. "I have told you that for a long time. I don't like your semen in my mouth. Even when I've tried to swallow it, I've ended up almost throwing up. Do you want me to vomit every time we have sex, Dom?"

I shrug my shoulders. "Maybe. If that's what it takes." My answer is arrogant and selfish and I know it. Even so, I let it permeate the air as Renee latches onto it and shakes her head.

"So vulgar. So rude." She turns and walks into the bathroom. I watch her go, but I do nothing to stop her. Renee will likely be in there for a while, if past arguments are any indication. I've upset her terribly and she will attempt to punish me by removing herself from my presence for a while. It works to a degree, but my heart is growing harder by the day. I'm worried that my callousness will eventually push us apart.

"Dammit," I say under my breath as I sit down on the edge of the bed. Though I'm angry at Renee for not trying harder, I do understand her plight. She loves me and she enjoys sex with me, but there are limitations. In some marriages, those limitations are fine between those two people. However, I want more from our sex life. I want her to swallow my jism. I want to fuck her in the ass. Is that really so much to ask from her? Perhaps it is, but I will continue to ask even as we get ready to leave for Nassau.

Chapter Three: Nassau

"It's gorgeous," Renee says with a smile as we walk into the beachside hotel. The ocean is within view as we make our way in.

"We have a view that faces the ocean," I tell her. "We'll be able to enjoy the sea air while we watch the sun go down in the evenings."

My wife nods her head. "I'm glad we're doing this, Dom. It's been too long since we last took a vacation. This will be such a nice rest."

A clerk greets us at a counter in the lobby. "Reservations?" She smiles widely as she looks at the two of us.

"Yes, for two. The Liggett's." I watch as the young woman looks at her computer screen for a moment.

"I have found your reservation, Mr. Liggett. A suite with a king bed?" I nod my head. "Then your room is ready for you." She reaches over and picks up two scan cards. The clerk quickly imprints them and then slides them into a small envelope before handing them over to me. "Room three-eleven. I hope you enjoy your stay in Nassau." The clerk motions for a young man nearby who comes toward us and takes our bags to place on a cart. After he does so, we make our way to the elevator and then upstairs to our room.

"Thank you," I say to the young man as he finishes putting our things inside the hotel room. I hand him a twenty-dollar bill and watch as he closes the door behind him. Turning, I can see that Renee has already made her way to the large sliding glass door at the other side of the room where there is a balcony with an ocean view. She goes outside and stands there while smiling.

"This is so nice, Dom," she tells me as she inhales the ocean air. "I don't think I'll want to go home at the end of this trip."

Chuckling, I reply, "Well, we have a solid week here, my love. Give it time. You might actually begin to miss home."

"Oh, I don't know." She turns and puts her arms around my shoulders, kissing me deeply as she does. Renee is a sensual woman, her love for me obvious as she runs her hands over the sides of my head. This is the sort of thing I was hoping for by taking a nice vacation with her. We need some time to help strengthen our intimacy with each other.

"I want to go snorkeling," Renee says as she leans her head back after the kiss. "I've never done that before."

"Me neither," I say with a laugh. "Sure, that sounds like it might be fun. We can see about setting that up for this week."

"Good." My wife takes my hand as she draws me back into the hotel room.

"And maybe some deep sea fishing. That's another thing I would love to try."

Renee frowns. "That doesn't sound like much fun, Dom."

"Not much fun? Have you seen some of those fishing shows? Honey, when you get a big fish on the line, it can be the fight of your life to reel it in."

My wife giggles. "I'll give you the fight of your life." She comes up to me again and we kiss hard. Her hands move all over me and I begin to wonder if we are about to have sex. Oh, hell, I want to fuck Renee. Unfortunately, she pulls back from me again and just smiles before walking around the hotel room. "We'll have to eat dinner soon. Where should we go for our first meal on the island?"

"Oh, I don't know. Maybe Pizza Hut."

Renee raises an eyebrow. "I didn't come all this way to just go to a Pizza Hut restaurant. They probably don't have one here anyway."

I laugh. "You don't want pizza?"

"Come on, Dom." We both laugh. I love to see my wife so happy and carefree. It's a nice change of pace from our time at work.

"I hope a client doesn't call while we're gone," Renee says as if she can read my mind about work.

"Not a chance. I sent emails out to everyone to let them know that the office is closed. Nothing pressing was on the calendar for the week, so we don't have to worry about anything, baby. Just relax." We've gotten so used to constantly being on call for our clients that it's easy for us to fixate on our responsibilities. I just hope that we can fully enjoy our time here instead of worrying about clients or work in general.

"Things happen," Renee replies. "That's how our line of work goes."

Nodding my head, I tell her, "I understand that, honey. Still, that's not likely to happen. Besides, most of them have my cell number. They can call me directly if they really have to."

"Probably during sex," my wife jokes. We laugh together.

"Yeah, sex." I recall what I said to Renee about our sex life and what I want to experience while we're on vacation. My comments raised a sore point for the both of us that I would have preferred to have left alone. I have to face up to the fact that my wife has limits as to what she feels she can do in bed. As her husband, I need to respect that line and keep from going over it. I love her deeply, after all.

Renee sits down on the sofa nearby. "You're happy with me, right?"

"Happy? Of course I'm happy, baby."

"No, not that. You know what I mean." My wife hasn't forgotten our conversation from last week either. "I know I'm not the loose whore you wish that I was, Dom. I try to be, but I keep fucking it up."

I sigh. "You're not fucking anything up. Renee, we are two different people. As a couple, we have to compromise. I have to learn to be more understanding of the way you feel about some things."

She smiles. "You're a pretty understanding guy. Maybe if I try to be more of the slut you want..."

"No, don't say that," I interrupt. "You're not a whore or a slut. Don't talk like that." It's the sort of thing that my wife will say whenever she's trying to make a harsh point. The point here being that I have been an asshole to her with the way I have pointed out what I see as her shortcomings sexually.

"I love you, though. I really do."

I walk over to the sofa and sit down beside her. "I love you too, honey. We are going to have a great time here, no matter what we do. We just need to pick a place to eat for this evening." I'm hoping that I can change the topic of our conversation so that Renee and I can move past what I said a few days ago.

She smiles. "Well, we're on an island with an ocean all around us. Shouldn't we go to a restaurant that reflects that? Or at least one that has local specialties?"

"Sure we should." I smile. "Downstairs while checking in I noticed that there's a hotel restaurant. We could go there for our meal tonight. I'll bet they have local cuisine on the menu."

"I'll bet they do," Renee says with a sweet smile. I enjoy seeing her beautiful blue eyes looking back at me. I truly am a lucky man when it comes to her. She wasn't my first choice, though, and she knows it. However, I didn't know my current wife when I proposed to a young woman named Tiffany Lawrence the year before Renee and I were engaged. It was a whirlwind romance, full of deeply passionate sex. Sometimes my wife suspects that I'm comparing her to Tiffany while we are having sex together. To some extent, that's probably true, though I attempt to keep from doing that as much as possible. I think it might be one reason why my wife is so hurt by my words when I share that I want sex to be more adventurous between us.

"So, what about the snorkeling thing? When would you like me to try to set that up?"

Renee looks down at her hands, both of them fidgeting around in her lap. Smiling and looking back up at me, she replies, "Maybe in a couple of days? I want to spend tomorrow just visiting the beach and walking around the island to get familiar with everything. What do you think?"

"I think we will do whatever you want to do," I tell her as I put my hand on top of hers. Renee grimaces. "What's wrong?"

"Whatever *I* want to do? Dom, what do *you* want to do while we're here? I'm not the only one on vacation." Her blue eyes look intently into mine.

I shrug. "I don't know. There's so much to do here, honey. I love to do whatever you want to do."

"No." Renee gets up from the sofa. Pacing around a little, I can see that she's bothered by something.

"What's wrong?" I ask.

"Nothing," she answers quickly. "Nothing at all. We should take a shower before the meal. After being on the flight, I feel a little icky." Renee walks over to where our bags are sitting and picks up one of hers. She carries it to the bed and puts it down, unzipping it to get into its contents.

"What's happening, my love? What did I say?" I'm confused by the sudden turn of our conversation.

"It's fine, Dom. Really." She feigns a smile as she looks for a change of clothes. "Do you want to shower first, or should I?"

"Come on, Renee. What's bothering you? You know you can tell me."

She sighs. "Honestly?" I nod my head. "Stop patronizing me, Dom. Just stop it. Don't do it. Ever. It's not always about what I want, you know." Her blue eyes, just moments ago soft and loving, are now accusatory and harsh.

"Patronizing? Because I said that I want to do whatever you want to do?"

"Yeah, that. You do it a lot. Stop doing it." I'm confused as she puts the clean clothes down on the bed and begins to take off what she's wearing so that she can take a shower.

"I'm sorry," I tell her softly. "I don't mean to patronize. I really do like doing whatever you want to do."

She shakes her head. "It makes me out to be the little queen, Dominique. I don't like to be thought of like that. I'm your wife, not your princess or boss. I can do whatever you want to do once in a while."

"Like deep sea fishing," I chuckle.

"Yeah, fine. I'll go deep sea fishing. Just stop telling me that you'll simply go along to do whatever I want to do. That just makes me feel worse than before."

"Worse than before?" My mind struggles to understand what she's talking about with this last comment. "What do you mean by before?"

Renee frowns. "The sex thing from a few days ago. You made me feel like shit when you said those things to me. It's like I don't make you happy." I know that what I said that day upset my wife, but I didn't realize that she has started tying it to other aspects of our life.

"I shouldn't have said those things," I reply. "Please forgive me for that and forget it. You're my wife and I love the way that you are. Everything about you makes me happy, Renee. Never forget that."

"Not everything, Dom. That's just another example of you patronizing me. It has to stop."

"And what am I supposed to say to you? Do I just keep insulting you? I told you that I made a mistake. Please understand, I didn't really mean those words, baby."

"Sure you did." Renee smirks a little. "Dom, you don't mince words when you're upset with me. The patronizing stops when you get pissed off, and I saw it the other day. You hate me for not swallowing and for not wanting anal sex. I know it. I can see it in your face whenever we have sex together. You have become bored with me."

"I'm not bored with you." The mood has completely changed suddenly in the hotel room.

"You're bored. I can see it in your face even now, Dominique. It's okay, though. I get it. I don't do some of the things that you want me to do." She offers a second faux smile before retreating into the bathroom with some things. Renee closes the door and I'm left behind to attempt to decipher how things turned dour so quickly.

"Fuck, Dom," I say to myself. "You are screwing everything up, aren't you?" Our vacation to Nassau is supposed to be a time for the two of us to enjoy each other. Instead, I feel as if the two of us are suddenly miles apart and I'm confused as to what to do to fix things. Shaking my head, I go back to the balcony and have a seat. Maybe the crisp ocean breeze will help to clear things up for me. If not, this entire trip could be difficult for Renee and I both.

Chapter Four: Similar Interests

"It's not black tie," I tell Renee as we make our way toward the hotel restaurant. "One of the hotel staff told me that they like the nicer beach stuff, which we have on. No bikinis or anything like that in the restaurant."

"That's good," Renee replies without looking at me. My heart sinks a little as I consider her demeanor after our little conversation in the hotel room earlier. If only we could have just made out and had sex instead of talking. The sort of sex that she prefers. I would have been happy to have done that. I love my wife and I don't like when she gets down like this. Unfortunately, it's my fault that she feels the way that she does right now.

"Good evening," an older gentleman says to us at the door of the restaurant. "How many?"

"Just the two of us," I tell him. "Liggett."

He scans a tablet on the podium in front of him. "Very well. Please follow me this way." He turns and picks up two menus before leading us to a table in the restaurant. As we walk in, I make note of the number of other tourists here. There are lots of couples and some families, many of whom are actively conversing and enjoying their meals together.

Here we are," the gentleman says to us. He pulls out my wife's seat and waits for her to sit down. I do the same on the other side of the small round table for myself. "I will have a server attend to you immediately." He bows his head before saying, "Enjoy your meal," and then walks away.

"Fancy enough," I say with a smile as I look around the restaurant. "Better than a Pizza Hut."

Renee allows a slight smile. "Much better." She opens her menu and I do the same. We both begin to scan through the offerings here and barely notice at first a young couple nearby who are watching us.

"Pardon me," the man says with a smile. I turn to look at him. "Are you both from the States?"

I nod my head. "Ohio."

"New Mexico." He reaches toward me and I reach back to take his hand. We shake. "It's good to meet you. My name is Simon Dumond and this is my wife Andrea." Simon is tall and good looking, his dark blond hair parted neatly to the right of his head. His blue eyes practically dance around as he smiles and nods toward my wife and I. His wife Andrea, also very attractive, has long brown hair and stunning hazel eyes. She smiles softly along with her husband as introductions are made.

"Dominique Liggett. This is my wife Renee."

"It's nice to meet you both," Andrea says as she looks from me to my wife. "How long have you been in Nassau?"

"Just arrived today," my wife replies. "This is our first dinner on the island."

"Oh, good." Andrea smiles warmly, her full lips stretching seductively in a way that causes me to imagine her gently syphoning my pecker. My mind quickly attempts to stifle such a thought as she continues, "The lobster bisque is amazing here."

"Lobster bisque?" I nod my head. "That sounds good to me."

"Yeah, it does," my wife agrees. "And how long have the two of you been here?"

"On and off?" Simon says. "It depends. This time around, we've been here for a couple of weeks. We own a place here where we stay, so our trips are sometimes more of the extended variety."

"And my husband can work wherever he wants. He's a tax attorney."

"Sweethcart, they probably don't want to hear that. The thing about lawyers and all."

"We're attorneys as well," I reply gladly. "Renee and I just opened our own firm a few months ago. I practice corporate law."

"How interesting." Simon smiles. "I tried my hand at that but it just wasn't my cup of tea. Taxes, though, I seem to have a gift for."

"A huge gift," his wife chimes in. "It's why we can travel so much." It's obvious that Andrea is proud of her husband. However, there's the slightest braggadocious tone to her voice. "And I'm an interior designer."

"Really?" Renee seems genuinely interested in this bit of information. "For personal homes?"

"Mostly," she replies. "I've designed a few Hollywood homes as well. Most of the time, it's just whatever I can do in New Mexico."

"Or in Nassau," Simon adds. "She has just finished the final touches on the island governor's home."

"Really? And this trip is a tax break for you?"

"Of course. Isn't yours?" Simon raises an eyebrow as I look over at Renee.

"See? We could write this thing off. We are having a nice conversation with another attorney at the moment and that counts. We could even talk to Andrea about decorating ideas for our own offices." Smiling, I'm glad to cause Renee's face to brighten up a little.

"Dom," she chuckles. "Seriously? He's a tax attorney. Of course he knows what to do to make his trip a deduction for his taxes."

"Shall we?" Simon waves his hand toward our table. I nod my head and he motions toward a server. "Could we move to their table?" The young woman nods and the Dumond's get up to join us as their chairs are moved over by the server.

"This is fun," I say as I look over at Renee. She nods her agreement as the two of them sit down at our table. "So, you live here part time?"

"Only occasionally," Andrea answers. "We are fairly free to come and go as we like to. This has only been over the last couple of years, though."

"Because of tax law and interior design?" Renee queries. "Maybe Dom and I are in the wrong business."

"Oh, no, it's not just because of that," Simon replies. "I actually inherited some money from my grandfather when he passed away two years ago. It was enough to make things very easy for us and I've also used some of it to grow my own law firm. There are a dozen other attorneys who work for me."

"And how old are you?" I ask while raising my eyebrows.

"Thirty-three."

"Damn. I'm only a year younger than you. I wish I had a wealthy grandfather that could leave me a few dollars." I realize how this sounds only after saying it. "I'm sorry, that's crass."

Simon laughs. "Nah, you're right. We honestly wouldn't be where we are right now had he not left me a sizable trust. It pays the bills here and at a place along the Mediterranean in the south of France."

"Seriously?" Renee looks at Andrea. "That must be so nice."

"It is." Andrea replies. "We have been very fortunate the last couple of years."

"Good evening," a server says to us. "Can I offer you some wine this evening to start off with?"

Simon looks at us. "Well? Do you like wine?"

"We love wine," I tell him.

He smiles and looks up at the server. "Do you have anything from Graycliff?"

"Always." The server nods her head.

"Bring us the best that you have. Leave the bottle here."

"Yes, sir." She nods before walking away.

"Graycliff? I haven't heard of it," I tell the other man.

"Graycliff is a world-renowned wine cellar in Nassau. It's very exclusive and very hard to get into for a meal."

"It's a thousand dollars per plate just to eat in the cellar near their wines," Andrea adds. "It's a wonderful place, though. Worth every penny."

"And the bottle of wine you just ordered?" Renee says with raised eyebrows.

"It's whatever they have. It will either be a red or white wine. Around ten thousand per bottle."

"Dollars?" I shake my head. "We weren't expecting to buy such an expensive bottle, Simon."

"You're not buying it," he tells me. "My wife and I are picking up the tab, Dominique. Don't worry." He smiles at me as if I'm an old friend.

How can a couple that we've just met drop so much money for our meal so easily?

"That's really too much," Renee tells them. "Maybe we can pay for part of it?"

"Don't be silly," Andrea tells her. "Honestly, Simon and I will cover this. We spend much more than this on many days here."

"Remember, it's a tax write off for me," Simon tells us. "This bottle will cost us next to nothing by the time I am finished with our taxes this quarter."

The server approaches the table and shows the bottle label to Simon. He nods his head and she pulls a corkscrew from her apron pocket. She begins to screw it into the top before quickly and sharply pulling it from the bottle. The server then puts a little in Simon's glass. He smells it for a moment before tasting a bit of it. Again, he nods his head and the server begins to fill the rest of our glasses.

"Very nice," Andrea remarks after she has a sip of the red wine. "Very sweet."

"Almost like the aroma of lilac as it crosses the tongue," her husband adds. "Put this on my account, please."

"Yes, Mr. Dumond," the young woman says before placing the bottle on the table. "Would you like to order, now?"

Simon looks at us. "May I?"

"Of course," Renee answers. Her eyes follow him as if she's mesmerized by the other man at the table. I'm a little surprised that she has so far gone along with this the way that she has.

"The lobster bisque for us all, please. Also, some of those wonderful breadsticks that you have here."

"Right away." The server gives us a slight nod before turning and walking away.

"You have an account here?" I say with incredulity.

Simon chuckles. "Like we said earlier, we're here a lot. They know me well enough to know that I pay my bills on time. They will send me a statement at the end of the week and I'll pay the tab then. It works out nicely." He raises his glass and says, "To the Liggett's from Ohio. May your stay here in Nassau be what you expect and then some."

"Here-here," Andrea adds as we all raise our glasses and then take a drink.

"So," Simon says as he puts down his glass. "What are your plans while here?"

"Snorkeling and maybe some fishing," I tell him. "We haven't really thought it all through just yet. I guess we're playing it by ear."

"I see," he replies. "Then, you just have to go out on the boat with us tomorrow."

"Boat? You have one here?" Renee leans forward, her arms on the table in front of her.

"We have a boat, sure," he answers. "And it's nice enough that we could go out tomorrow on the ocean and enjoy ourselves. Maybe bring along some wine and a picnic lunch as well."

"It's great fun out there," Andrea says. "Please say yes."

"Yes, of course," my wife answers without waiting on me to say anything. I did, after all, tell her that I would be happy to do whatever she wants to do. As patronizing as I was probably being, I meant every word of it. However, we don't know these people all that well. They have told us who they are and how they have come into some money, but can we be completely certain that they're not the sort that will take us out on the ocean and then rob us before dumping us overboard? It wouldn't take much to make someone disappear, after all. Not in the ocean.

"So, on your boat? Where's it at?"

"It's named after my wife and it's docked in the south of the island. I'll text you the exact location and you can both meet us there in the morning. How does ten o'clock sound?"

"We'll be there," Renee answers swiftly. "Thank you so much for the invitation!"

"It's our pleasure," he replies.

"And you'll love the lobster bisque," Andrea promises. "You'll never look at lobster the same way again."

"Good." I smile and nod my head as I study both of our new acquaintances. Renee seems enthralled with them, and I suppose that's a good thing. Even so, there's something about them that I can't quite put my finger on. For some reason they decided to open a conversation with us, even though we're complete strangers. Why? And why are they paying for our drinks and meals? Perhaps that will become apparent tomorrow as we go out on their boat with them. I just hope it has some kind of covering to keep Renee and I from getting sunburned. We are from Ohio, after all, and we still don't have sunscreen.

Chapter Five: A Closer Bond

31

"This is not just a boat," I say as Renee and I board the *Andrea Leanne.*

"Are you sure this is the right one?" my wife asks as her eyes take in the large yacht. "I mean, they said they had a *boat,* but this is a lot more like a full scale ship."

My wife and I have seen yachts before. On Lake Erie last year while visiting a relative we saw several smaller yachts. I would never consider any of those the ocean-going sort. At least not with the ability to cross the entire ocean or a Great Lake. No, what sits here is large and very imposing.

"Welcome aboard," Andrea says to us as we reach the top of the steps. "What do you think?"

"You're serious, right?" Renee shakes her head. "You're not joking around about this being your boat?"

"Of course not." The other woman seems confused as she looks at my wife and I. "We don't joke about this sort of thing." She smiles as she looks around. "I know it's a bit much, but don't worry. We've hired a capable captain and crew to take us out. Simon rarely does any of the operating of our boat near the port. He doesn't have his captain's license yet."

"Wow." I shake my head as I look at the beautiful wooden deck. It has to cost a lot just to maintain a vessel of this size.

"Good morning!" Simon comes out onto the deck from a door nearby. "I see you've met the *Andrea Leanne.*"

"A giant yacht," I chuckle. "It's huge."

"Ah, yes. It's a yacht, but not as large as some."

"But it's larger than most, Simon. You have to admit that much."

He smiles wide. "My grandfather owned another yacht and when I sold it we had just enough to buy this one. I thought about naming it after him, but calling it *Gerald* just didn't have the same ring to it as using my lovely wife's name." Simon walks over to Andrea and takes her into his arms. They kiss passionately as Renee and I stand by and watch.

"Sweetie, our guests," Andrea says as she blushes a few moments later.

"Oh, sorry," he chuckles. "I get carried away sometimes. I'll bet that happens to the two of you occasionally."

I look over at Renee. She says nothing, so I reply, "Sure, yeah. We get a little carried away a lot." My response sounds mildly corny and disingenuous to me, but our hosts don't seem to notice as they begin to lead us toward the cabin.

"Let's give you a grand tour." We walk inside the large sliding glass doors just as the yacht begins to back away from the dock. "This is our lounge area, complete with a six-person jacuzzi," Simon says as he motions his hands around the room. "There is a small bar, sometimes worked by a bartender whom we borrow from a local pub. Over there are leather seats and a sixty-inch television." We make our way to the bar area and he steps behind it. "How about a lemon mint spritzer?"

"Alcohol? This early?" Renee says.

"Oh, no, this is a mocktail," Andrea replies. "It's really good, though. A great vitamin C drink for the morning." My wife nods her head and Simon begins to add the ingredients to a shaker.

"So, how many people can you put on this yacht at one time?" I ask as I take a seat at the bar.

Simon shrugs as he works on the drinks. "I think we've had around fifty people on the boat once before. Maybe a few more. It was a party last Christmas."

"It was a great party," his wife adds. "And there was plenty of room. With six bathrooms and eight sleeping berths, it's a pretty comfortable way to party."

"That's incredible," I say with a laugh. Simon slides a tall glass of the lemon mint spritzer toward me.

"Take a quick sip of that and tell me if it's good."

I do as he asks. "That's amazing," I say as I hand it over to Renee so she can try a taste of it.

"Really amazing. You should be a bartender."

Simon laughs. "It doesn't pay nearly enough." He works on three more glasses of the light yellow concoction with mint leaves before walking out from behind the bar. He and his wife then lead us to the leather seats nearby where we sit down and begin to talk.

"So, what do the two of you do for fun?" Andrea asks.

"Well, this is fun," Renee says with a smile after taking another sip of her mocktail.

"Besides this. What do you both do when you're looking for fun things to do in Ohio?"

"Hiking and visiting Lake Erie, I suppose," I reply to her. "Sometimes we like to take in a movie or go visit friends and family."

"We like some of those things too," Simon interjects. "Though we don't see family very often. We have plenty of friends in Nassau, though." He takes a drink from his glass. "It's hard to find really close friends around here, though."

"Close friends." I nod my agreement. "We really don't have very many close friends back home. At least, not the sort of friends who like to get together and have really serious personal conversations."

Andrea sighs. "We would love to have closer friends, but you never know if their interests align with yours, you know? We've had other people on our boat before, and to be honest, most of them just left and never came back when the day was over. It's been really disappointing."

I suddenly feel as if my wife and I are interviewing for the positions of head best friends with our hosts. It's a weird feeling to know that someone is looking at you and considering whether you are of the right quality to fulfill whatever expectations they have of you. I wonder if we're snooty enough for them? Sure, Renee and I are attorneys, but not filthy rich attorneys. Simon and Andrea probably spend more money in a week than my wife and I make in a month at our law practice.

"That being said, what do the two of you like to do with close friends? At least, if you had close friends? What would you like to do?" Simon puts his drink down in a cup holder in the arm of his chair.

"I don't know," I begin as I look at my wife for help to answer the question. "Probably a lot of the same things that we already do. It would be nice to take hikes and visit beaches with close friends. It would be nice to also have someone we could call and talk to freely.

Andrea nods her head. "We want to be close friends with you both, but if we are, we want to know more about you. It's our belief that the more we know about our friends, the closer we can be with them. Wouldn't you agree?" The young woman's breasts bulge at the top of her tight tee shirt as she sits back in her seat. It makes me a little hard as I imagine what they look like without all the material covering them.

"I can agree with that," Renee replies. "The more you know about someone, the better you can relate to them."

"Exactly!" Simon says as he pulls up his shirt. He lifts it over his head to reveal his smooth, muscular chest. I can see that he has Renee's attention as he turns slightly and points to a scar on the back of his shoulder. "I caught a piece of metal in my back one time when a lawn mower exploded."

"*What?*" I try to keep myself from laughing a little, but the statement seems too fantastic. "How did you end up that close to a lawn mower?"

"I wasn't always rich," Simon begins to explain. "I worked for my Uncle Chris in a lawn business when I was sixteen. Unfortunately, he had a guy who worked for him cutting grass. He was high on meth a lot of the time and didn't make very good decisions. Well, one day while the mower was still hot after cutting grass, he decided to refill the tank with gasoline. Some of the fuel got onto the hot engine and it ignited. Then the fuel tank caught fire and before I could get away it blew up. He died and I ended up with a two-by-three inch hunk of metal in my shoulder."

"Shit," I say while shaking my head. "Did you get it out?"

"My uncle used a pair of pliers to pull it out right before the ambulance got there for the other guy. He paid me a thousand bucks to keep it a secret from my parents. To this day, they don't know about this scar."

"You didn't go to the doctor?"

"Oh, I did, but he was a friend of Uncle Chris. He kept his mouth shut too." Simon smiles as he looks over at Andrea. "Your turn, my sweet." I get hard as I look at his wife. I'm hoping that she will be removing some clothing as well.

"It's always hard to follow up after that story, but here I go," Andrea says before telling us, "I used to be a prostitute." There's a dead silence in the room as my wife and I process what she's told us.

"Um, what?" Renee's eyes grow wide.

"A hooker," Andrea says. "I know it sounds pretty scandalous, but I was a high-class escort in Albuquerque before I met Simon. As a matter of fact, that's *how* we met." She smiles as she reaches over and takes her husband's hand. "He came to see me as a client and we both realized just how much we enjoyed sex together. From there on I quit my job and moved in with him."

"That's different," I chuckle. "I would not have ever guessed."

"I've removed myself from that time in my life," Andrea tells us. "But we still enjoy and active sex life. Do the two of you have a great sex life?" The question surprises both me and Renee as we sit and look at each other.

"Um, we have sex," Renee answers. "Like most married people."

"But *good* sex?" Simon sits back in his chair and puts one leg on top of the other. "The kind that other people might be amazed to see? We're talking about satisfying bouts of passion."

My guess is that Simon has crossed his legs because he's getting an erection from this conversation. I also find myself having to move around to keep the others in the room from seeing the growing bulge inside my own pants. For new acquaintances, they are really bold in their conversation with us. What is it that they really are hoping to do with us here?

"We have good sex," Renee says before taking a nervous drink of lemon mint spritzer.

"I can see that," Andrea replies while nodding her head. "Anyway, we don't mean to press. We just like to talk." She looks over at her husband and says, "We should go out on deck and enjoy the ocean before having some lunch, don't you think?"

"Yeah, let's do that." Simon puts his tee shirt back on and he leads us to the deck of the large yacht. As we walk out of the cabin, I think about what we have been talking about. Our hosts must be very openly sexual people, ready to enjoy the company of someone else if given the opportunity. Are they on the hunt for other lovers? Who knows. For now, we'll simply enjoy the voyage along the coastline of Nassau.

Chapter Six: Wounded

"That was really out there," Renee says to me as we get back to our hotel room. My wife moves toward the sofa on one side of the room and has a seat before turning on the television.

"Yeah, it was something," I agree. "I'm guessing that they are pretty open about talking about sex, huh?"

She nods her head. "I guess so." I watch my wife remove her sandals and pull her feet onto the sofa with her. Something bothers her.

"Are you alright?" I ask.

"I'm fine," she replies flatly. "It was just a crazy day. You know, I don't know that I want to spend any more time with them, Dom. Maybe we should just focus on each other during or vacation."

"Um, okay." I sit down beside her on the sofa. "Are you angry at them for some reason? Did one of them say something rude to you on the yacht?"

Renee shakes her head. "No, not really. Nothing that I care to rehash. It's all good. I just want to spend a little more time with just the two of us, babe. That's all." My wife manages a quick smile before she turns her attention back to the television. However, I don't want to let this go so easily. After all, the Dumond's seem like a nice couple. They're a lot like us in many ways.

"Look, they are pretty free when talking about sex. That bothers you, and I'm cool with not talking about that sort of thing with them. We just need to let them know that's off limits for now."

My wife turns her brilliantly blue eyes toward me. "You wanted to tell them, didn't you? I could see it in your face, Dom. You wanted to tell Simon and Andrea that I'm a terrible sex partner."

"What? Of course not!"

"Don't deny it, dammit. I'm not a child. You and I both know that you're not happy with our sex life. We don't have the sort of passionate sex that they have. It's obvious." Renee pulls her feet out from under her and then stands up from the sofa. She walks over to a small refrigerator and pulls out a bottle of water from inside.

"I didn't say anything to them and I didn't want to," I tell her. "They're nice people but a little quirky. I never planned to say a thing about any of our personal disagreements."

"Our *disagreements,*" she parrots. "What a way to say that you want me to do things that you know that I can't. Dammit, Dominique. Why are you so driven by a desire to fuck me in the ass or have me swallow your semen?"

"Honey, we're already past that. I'm not blaming you for anything. I'm not disappointed with you at all." Of course, I'm lying to Renee. I am pretty disappointed that my own wife won't at least suck me off to completion and try a little harder to swallow my spunk. That doesn't mean that I don't love her more than anyone else in the world and would do anything for her.

"We're not past it. You would have told them all about it if I hadn't been there with you. I saw how you were looking at Andrea. You would screw her in a heartbeat if you could." The Dumond's sexual remarks didn't end when we left the cabin and went out on deck. They continued to drop hints as to what they do in bed together and what they enjoy together. For our part, we simply continued to tell them that we have a healthy sex life. Andrea seemed very perceptive as she watched my reaction to the conversation. Perhaps that's what Renee noticed as well.

"Look, I'm not making any sort of fuss about our sex life, honey. As far as I'm concerned, the conversation with them is over." Sighing, I decide to let her have her way. "Fine, we won't see the Dumond's again. You and I will have this vacation just between the two of us exactly the way you want it."

Renee glares at me. "You're patronizing me again, aren't you?"

"For fuck's sake, sweetheart, I'm just *agreeing* with you. Why are you being like this?"

"Like what? Like an uptight *prude?* That's really what you wanted to tell Andrea, isn't it? You wanted to say that Simon was a lucky man that his wife loves to give blow jobs and swallow. Why didn't you just say that?" She walks over to me and hands me a business card that Simon gave her while on the yacht. "Go ahead and call them, Dominique. Tell them what a terrible lover I am. Tell them how I disappoint you and you have to patronize me just to get along with me. You might earn some brownie points with her and get a real blow job from a real woman."

"That's enough!" I back away and refuse to take the small business card from my wife. "Stop doing this, Renee. Sure, I suppose I sometimes patronize you. I'm sorry for that and I honestly don't mean to do it. But whenever you get into this nasty mood you blow things way out of proportion. So, you stop doing that and I'll stop patronizing you. How about that?" I shake my head as I get up off the sofa and walk toward the bed. I'm tired and my lower back hurts a little. It might be nice to relax for a while.

"Really? You're the one who is disappointed, Dom. You're the one who can't seem to be happy with what you have with me. Regular sex isn't what you want, huh? Vanilla sex sucks. Isn't that what you said one time last year?"

"For fuck's sake."

"You remember that, right? When you and I were at the New Year's Eve party with my friends and family? You griped to one of my cousins about vanilla sex? I think he found that pretty damned funny."

"I was a little tipsy," I reply in my defense. "You can't blame me for what I said after having a few drinks, Renee. Besides, he didn't remember any of it after that party. He was already drunk out of his mind when we talked about that."

"Oh, you told me that, but we both know better. He remembered it. Jase doesn't look at me the same way anymore, Dominique." It's likely that my dear wife is correct. Her cousin Jase might remember what I said to him about our lackluster time in bed together. Even if he does, it doesn't matter. It was just two drunk dudes having a really stupid conversation.

"You're wearing me the fuck out," I tell her. "Just give it a rest and lie down with me for a while. We're both tired."

"No, I don't think so." Renee frowns as she shakes her head. She goes to the bathroom and closes the door behind her.

"I'm sorry," I call out to her. "Really, I am." My voice sounds less than convinced of my own attempt to smooth things over. If I'm completely honest with myself, my wife has been less than great in bed for a long time. However, I've been more than patient over the years and tried to help her get over her reservations about both oral and anal sex. I would love to see some movement in either one, but Renee isn't ready to give in. This has become more of a shoving match between us and she intends to win. For a long time I was willing to give up my sexual desires, but with the way she's behaving now, I'm beginning to have second thoughts.

The bathroom door suddenly opens. Renee steps to the doorway and simply stares at me. "You know, you can just spend this vacation on your own if you prefer, Dominique. We don't have to be together all the time if I bother you so much."

"How the hell...how am I sending any message to you that I'm bothered by you, Renee? I don't get this reaction to the Dumond's. Why are you being this way?"

Tears begin to fill her eyes as she runs her fingers through her blonde hair. "You don't want to be honest, do you? We both know what you think of me. Don't act like I can't see what's going on." Renee turns and walks toward the door. After picking up her small purse, she opens the hotel room door and then leaves. The room is eerily quiet as I get up from the bed and try to understand what the hell is going on.

"Is this really happening?" I ask myself as I begin to regret taking this trip in the first place. Though we are supposed to be on vacation, it feels like anything but a time away from work. On the contrary, I feel as if I'm being raked over the coals here in Nassau. I wonder if either Simon or Andrea have had the same feelings between each other as Renee is having with me. If so, they don't show it. No, they seem to be an almost perfect couple in every way. They're happy and sexually satisfied. I'm a little jealous, truth be known. I would like our marriage to be more like theirs.

"I want to fuck Andrea," I chuckle to myself. "Yep, she'd swallow. Then she'd let me fuck her in the ass." My eyes turn toward the closed hotel room door. "Andrea would make me happy, Renee. She wouldn't turn me down for anal sex and she would probably never say the things you have said to me." There's a bit of anger that is rising inside me as I think about my wife's behavior this afternoon. She obviously blames me for her unhappiness too. That bothers me more than the fact that our sex life literally sucks. Or, maybe it doesn't. That's the fucking problem. "Andrea sucks."

I smile to myself as I try to make light of my situation with Renee. Reaching for my hotel room card, I cup it into my hand and then slide it into my pocket. Opening the door, I soon enter the same hallway where my wife walked moments earlier. If she can storm out of the room and do whatever, so can I. Maybe a drink or two at the bar downstairs will help to smooth out my thoughts. Heaven knows it can't hurt, especially since Renee is so angry with me. I'm only bothered that I'll have to sit alone and drink. She's not here to enjoy a visit to the bar with me. Oh, well. I don't give a fuck anymore. It's just been one of those days, I suppose.

Chapter Seven: A Different Kind of Offer

I walk into the hotel bar and approach the bartender. After ordering a Coke and whiskey, I turn and look around at the other patrons in the room. A hand goes up and my eyes turn to the man to whom it belongs. It's Simon. After nodding my head in his direction, I put money down on the bar and walk over to where he's sitting.

"Well, look at who has come in for a drink." Simon grins at me as I sit down in a chair at his small table. "I guess we had the same idea, huh?"

"I guess so," I answer with a strained smile. I had hoped to spend some time wallowing in self-pity alone with my drink, but there was no way I could just ignore my new friend when he waved at me.

"So, how are things going this fine evening?" he asks.

I shrug my shoulders. "Just fine." I take a drink from my glass as I look around. "Do you frequent here often?"

"Sometimes," Simon replies. "It's good to get away from my wife and just think things through sometimes. Is that why you're here?" He lifts a glass of what appears to be dark beer and takes a sip.

"I guess you could say that," I answer. "Renee left the room, so I figured I would come in here and check out the bar." I turn to look at the decor of the bar. It's classy but not so classy that I feel like I need to dress better than I am already dressed.

"Andrea and I came by Renee a few minutes ago. The ladies decided to spend some girl time together for a while."

Surprised, I ask, "Did Renee say anything?"

"Like what?" Simon smiles.

"Well, like what she was doing when you came upon her. Was she okay?"

The other man's eyes study my facial expression. "Your wife seemed a little down. Just like you do right now, Dom. What's going on with you two? Did we say something offensive on the boat? If so, I would love to apologize to the both of you."

"Oh, no, you didn't say anything to offend either of us," I tell him. "My wife and I just have some issues we need to resolve between us, that's all. Honestly, you and Andrea were very cordial today."

Simon chuckles. "I'm not sure that cordial is the word for it. We allowed ourselves to get a little too free with our conversation."

"Free?"

"Of course. The sex thing. I'm very sorry about that, but my wife and I tend to be very open about that sort of thing and we went too far with it as it concerns you and Renee. I wish we had been a bit more delicate in our manners."

"No, it was us. Honestly." After a moment of thought, I tell him, "We've not had a great sex life for a long time. Renee and I don't see eye to eye when it comes to what we want to do in the bedroom. She was probably a little bothered by the talk of sex because of that. It really doesn't have much to do with you or Andrea." I can feel my face heating up as it turns red under the gaze of the other man. Though I probably shouldn't share this information with him, I feel that some explanation needs to be given in order for him to have a better perspective as to what is going on.

"Do you love each other?" Simon asks.

"Of course. Very much," I reply. "We are probably more in love now than ever before."

"But, you're not having the sort of sex that you want to have?"

I sigh. "It comes down to some of the things that often goes along with sex." I swallow hard as I gather my thoughts. It's a little embarrassing to share this sort of thing with another man that I've only just met. "You see, Renee is fine with straight sex. I sometimes refer to it as vanilla sex. She enjoys that as much as I do. However, if it comes to anything more than that, she's not as receptive to the idea."

"Oral?" I shake my head. "And anal?" Simon frowns as I shake my head for a second time. "Does she like oral performed upon her?"

"Definitely," I answer. "She loves it. As a matter of fact, she expects it most of the time."

"But, she doesn't like to do it to you?"

Shaking my head, I reply, "She'll start to do it and then when I'm getting off she'll pull it out of her mouth. She doesn't like for me to finish in there." I look around us to see if anyone is sitting close enough to hear our conversation. Renee would kill me if she thought I was sharing this information with several other people. It's bad enough that Simon and I are engaging in this sort of talk.

"I see." He frowns again. "Andrea and I have been full partners in everything having to do with sex. Practically anything goes as long as it's safe and approved by us both. Vaginal intercourse, anal intercourse, oral, BDSM..."

"Um..." I motion toward someone who has just sat down nearby.

Simon smiles. "You see, Dominique, I'm not so worried about that sort of thing. Andrea and I are very free in what we do." He turns and looks at the man who has just sat down nearby. "Excuse me, friend. Do you have anal sex with your significant other?"

The other man's eyebrows rise. "Uh, sometimes?" He seems pretty surprised by the question, as am I.

"Thank you. I was just wondering." Simon turns back to look at me. "You both have to let go and give in to your passions. Don't worry about what other people think of you or what you do together."

I sigh as I ask, "What do I do? How do I convince her to do more with me?"

Simon pulls his cell phone out of his shorts pocket. "You know, my wife and I haven't always been so willing to do things as freely as we are now. It took a change in how we interact with others." He pulls a video up on the screen and pushes it toward me. I pick up the cell phone and watch the video for a moment.

On the screen is Simon and Andrea, both naked, on a bed with another man and woman. They are having sex with each other, Andrea being fucked by the other man as Simon's dick is siphoned by the other woman. This goes on and on, the four fleshy bodies rolling around each other until they all orgasm. My cock stiffens as I hand the phone back to him.

"You see, things changed for us on this night. We had a foursome with another couple. It was here that for the first time my wife and I gave in to our desires for other people. We had a great time and it opened a new understanding of our sexual needs and desires."

"How did you convince Andrea?"

He chuckles. "She convinced me. Remember, my lovely wife was an escort at one time. She already had been given the opportunity to be with more than one lover at a time. I was the one in the relationship who was holding out for a while."

"But, were you as resistant as Renee is? She won't hardly give me a blow job at all and anal sex just isn't on the menu for us. I don't dare ask for it."

"There needs to be others who help you to convince her." Simon grins widely. "Andrea is likely having this same conversation with her right now. She might even be showing her the same video." He leans toward me. "We would very much enjoy spending some quality time with the two of you, if you know what I mean."

I swallow hard. "You mean, you want to have sex with us?" He nods his head. "Is that why you invited us to your yacht?"

Simon chuckles. "It is part of the reason. However, when we saw how difficult it was for Renee to discuss sex, we quickly pushed that thought out of our heads. You see, we never try to force people into things. We only offer and see if they agree to be a part of our passion."

"Renee would never do that."

"Wouldn't she? I don't think you give her the credit that she deserves, Dominique. Renee is a special woman, full of her own capability to enjoy sex. All she really needs is the right motivation and guidance."

"And you can give her that?"

"My wife and I can give that to the both of you." Simon smiles as he looks into my eyes. "Andrea and I have discussed this at length. We think we would all four be a wonderful match in bed. She is very interested in getting to know you better."

My cock stiffens as I consider what he's talking about. Sex with him and his wife. A sort of swapping of partners. I find Andrea striking and very sexually appealing, but I wonder if my wife would say the same of Simon? Sure, she's probably attracted to him in a way, but is she willing to let go and simply enjoy sex to its fullest? Would she be willing to let another man penetrate her sweet pussy and possibly her tight asshole? I'm not sure that she would. However, I've been wrong about things before. I could be wrong about this.

"I'm not sure what to say," I tell him. "What you're offering isn't the sort of thing that Renee and I have been offered before. I don't think we've even discussed this before."

"Maybe not, but it would be life changing for both of you, Dominique. It's a rare opportunity to get to experience passion in this way with other people. I think you would come to appreciate it greatly." Simon smiles. "Just think about it, alright?" He waves at a server nearby and she comes to the table. "Could you bring me another beer, please?"

She picks up the empty glass. "Absolutely, Mr. Dumond." The woman turns and walks away.

"I don't think Renee will agree to this," I tell him.

"But *you* would?" He raises an eyebrow as he smiles a little.

"I don't know," I answer as I try to get a grip on what I'm saying to the man. "Renee might not like that I've talked to you about this at all."

"We've gone over this already," he tells me. "Andrea is having the same sort of conversation with her. Would you be willing to consider having sex with my wife, Dominique? Do you want to have sex with her?" The question causes my heart to race as I think about Andrea. Of course I would love to have sex with her, but how do I admit as much to her husband? Also, could this be some kind of trick? Did my wife set me up by having Simon meet me in the bar? No, that can't be it. He has a video of him and his wife with another couple. Renee didn't know that I would come here, either. What should I tell him?

"Maybe," I answer cautiously. "It would depend upon what my wife says, Simon. I can't tell you that I would do something without knowing what she wants."

"Ah, you're one of those," he says jokingly. "A guy who leaves it all up to his wife. You put it all on Renee to decide what you want or desire. That might be part of the problem."

"I don't do that."

"Oh, don't you? Come on, Dominique. You can tell me what you want without checking with her first. Would you like to screw Andrea or not?" His face becomes firm as he gazes into my eyes. Simon wants an answer from me and he's not going to wait for me to check with my wife.

"Yes, I would. Okay? You've gotten it out of me." I feel a little irritated that I've had to admit that I want to fuck Andrea, but here we are.

"I'm glad that you could finally admit that." Simon smiles as he looks up at the young server who has arrived with his fresh beer. "Thank you, my dear." He hands her a twenty-dollar bill and smiles as she turns and walks away.

"And it doesn't bother you?"

He sips his beer for a moment before answering, "Not in the least. It excites me, Dominique. I think it will excite Andrea as well." Simon finishes off his beer pretty quickly as I continue to nurse the Coke and whiskey in my own glass. After a few minutes, he says to me, "I'm going to head back to my room now. I would think that Renee will be returning to your room shortly."

"Yeah, probably," I say as I nod my head.

"Thanks for the talk, Dominique. You have given me a lot to think about with Andrea."

"Yeah, you've given me something to think about as well." I shake my head and chuckle. "If it's true that Andrea has had this same conversation with Renee, things might be weird with my wife."

"Sure, that could be true," he says to me while standing to his feet. "But I think you'll find that she will have a different perspective. Andrea is very good at that." Simon gives me a quick wink before turning and walking away. For my part, I continue to sit in the bar for a few more minutes as I think about what we have talked about.

"Will Renee really change her mind?" I ask myself quietly. The larger part of me would like to answer no to this question, but I honestly can't be so certain. Perhaps Andrea is very good at convincing people to do things that they would normally not do. I'm sure Renee will probably have something to say about it back in the hotel room. Eager to find out, I get up and finish off my drink before leaving the bar.

Chapter Eight: The Possibilities

52

When I return to the hotel room my wife is already there. Renee is sitting on the balcony while quietly staring out at the ocean. I walk through the sliding glass door to see her.

"Hey," I say quietly as I sit down in the other chair on the balcony.

"Hey," she answers back without looking over at me. Her blue eyes are affixed on the rolling surf nearby. There's a storm out at sea that is currently pushing larger waves against the beach. It would likely not be the best time to go for a swim beneath the moonlight.

"I went to the bar," I tell her as I attempt to begin our needed conversation. "Simon was there." Renee finally looks over at me. "We had a talk about a few things."

Renee's face turns a little pink as she looks back out at the water. "I'll bet I can guess what you talked to him about."

I purse my lips for a moment. What if the conversation she had with Andrea wasn't exactly a pleasant one? What if my wife is now even angrier than before about our sex life issues and what I might or might not have said to someone? I don't think I can fucking take any more of the negativity that has invaded our recent conversations. It's causing some terrible bruising to our marriage.

"What did Andrea say?" I ask her as I try to turn the lead over to her.

An almost snide chuckle comes from my wife. "Well, apparently you've been right all along, Dom. I really am a terrible wife when it comes to sex. I've been holding out on you." Her face is dour as she shakes her head and sighs.

"Just tell me what she said," I say again. "You can tell me, honey. It's okay."

Renee turns to face me. "Andrea told me that I should be willing to give in to what you want any time you want it," she says as she grimaces. "She says that you have been very sweet to me and patient, but that it could eventually change."

"What does that mean?"

"I don't know. Why don't you tell me?" My wife glares at me coldly as I attempt to understand what the women must have said to each other.

"Honey, we've already hashed this out, right? We've talked about what I would like during sex. I think we know where we each stand."

"And I'm holding us back, huh? I'm the bad one in the marriage who's keeping you from having the sex that you want. Isn't that right, Dominique? Am I the one holding you back?" Though she sounds angry, I get the feeling that instead my wife feels crushed or defeated. What could Andrea have said that would make her so down?

"You're not holding anyone back," I reply. "Did she talk meanly to you? Simon seemed to think that Andrea would be a good person for you to speak with, Renee."

She nods her head. "Andrea was nice enough about it, but then she said that she would give you a great blow job and anal sex if I couldn't do it." This revelation causes my cock to swell as I shake my head.

"I can't believe that she said that to you."

"Well, she did," Renee retorts. "She fucking did."

"And would you want to have sex with Simon?" I don't know why I ask this, but I do. Something inside me feels like I need to press on and try to get to where something in our sex life gives a little.

"Are you serious?" she asks. "Did he say that he wanted to do that with me?"

"Yeah, he did," I answer while nodding my head. "They want to get with us for a foursome, Renee. Or, at least, some sort of swapping."

"Shit." My wife looks back out over the water, her mouth agape just a little as she considers what I've told her. "Andrea said she wanted to have sex with you, but she didn't say she wanted both couples to get together."

"Honey, it's okay. I didn't take Simon all that seriously either. We don't have to see them again if you would prefer not to. We'll work out our problems together."

"Don't patronize me again." Renee turns to face me as she frowns. "You do that all the time. It's always about what I want and never about what you want, Dom. Tell me what you want. Do you want to fuck her? Do you want to have sex with Andrea Dumond?"

The question sends chills down my neck as I stare back quietly at my wife. How do I answer this? To say that I do want to have sex with Andrea would surely cause Renee to doubt my love for her. However, to respond with a lie might lead her to believe that I'm still trying to patronize her in some way. Either option is likely unpalatable as I consider them.

"She's attractive," I admit as my body shudders.

"And you'd like to fuck her. Just be honest with me, Dom. Tell me the truth."

Swallowing hard, I reply, "I wouldn't turn down sex with her if I could have it." The answer is obvious, but short of sounding as if I'm asking Renee whether I can have sex with the other woman. However, being diplomatic has become a bit of a downfall in my marriage to my wife.

"So, you want to go to their yacht and have sex with them?"

"What?"

"Tonight. She invited you to come to their yacht at midnight, Dom. She wants you." Renee's blue eyes continue to glare at me as she considers that I am attracted to the other woman.

"I don't know. Do you feel attracted to Simon?" Renee suddenly turns away, her face turning red once again. "Holy shit. You are attracted to him, aren't you? Honey, do you want to have sex with him?"

"Sex with another man? Why? Is that a fetish of yours?" Renee is defensive in her answer to me. It doesn't surprise me at all, though. She often becomes defensive whenever I speak to her about sexual things.

"Maybe it is," I say firmly. "So what? You want to have sex with Simon. I can see that so clearly now. So, why are we having this conversation?"

Renee looks over at me. "Do you really think that another man can convince me to do the things that I don't want to do, Dominique? Do you think that Simon can get me to suck a dick and swallow? Is that what he told you?"

"Not exactly," I shoot back immediately. "If you have a different man with you in bed, though, things could happen in a way that helps you with that."

"All men are horny and think with their dicks," Renee says in disgust. "All fucking men."

"And what about women? Aren't some women the horny type as well? Andrea seems to be horny." Though comparing my wife to her is probably not the smartest thing for me to do, I want to be certain that I make my point. "You want Simon, don't you? Even for vanilla sex or whatever else he's willing to do with you."

"Fuck, Dominique…"

"Stop making this all about me," I interrupt. "You've shit on me over and over about what my needs and desires are during sex. I'm sick of feeling guilty about asking for something like a good blow job to completion and swallowing. Why can't I ask my wife for that?"

"Or Andrea." My wife has always had a quick wit.

"Either way, we both want more. Though you might want something other than more physical elements of sex, you still want something more from sex. Don't you?"

Her jaw flexes as she purses her lips and gets up from the chair. Renee walks back into the hotel room from the balcony and I get up to follow her. I won't allow her to leave this conversation so easily this time.

"So, you want to go at midnight to meet them?"

I take a quick breath before answering. "Yes, I do. I want to see what this might be like, Renee. You should want to go, too."

"Wow." She folds her arms and turns to face me. "If we do this, it will change everything. You know that, right?"

"Yeah, I know," I reply. "And I'm hoping that it will change everything for the better, my love. You and I both deserve to get what we want during sex, don't we? Couldn't you agree with that?"

Renee looks at me, her eyes filled with a few tears. "I'm scared, Dom. I don't want to lose you."

I walk over to my wife and take her into my arms. "You know what? I said for better and for worse in my marital vows to you, baby. I meant every word of it. It wouldn't matter if we suddenly quit having sex, I would never walk away from you. You're everything to me, Renee. Everything. I sometimes wish that you could see that." She wraps her arms around me and we quietly hold each other tightly.

"At midnight," she says quietly as she pulls away from me and wipes her eyes. "Andrea said that she would be waiting on the yacht with Simon if you want to have sex with her. I guess we'll both be going." She swallows hard and tells me, "I don't know that I want sex, but I can at least offer it to you. Andrea will give you what you want, Dom. I'm going to let you have it."

"But honey," I say while shaking my head. "I can't just do that in front of you."

"I want you to do this for me," Renee answers. "Promise me that when we go there tonight you will have sex with Andrea. Promise me that you will let her give you head and maybe even have anal sex with her."

"Holy shit," I mutter as I look into my wife's eyes. "Is that really what you want?"

"Yeah, it is," Renee replies. "Promise me that."

I sigh before saying, "Okay. I promise. I'll do it if you want."

"Don't patronize me," she says gently. "Do it because *you* want to do it, not because you think that it will make me happy, Dominique. I want to see you happy."

"Okay." We hug again before Renee pulls away and goes to the bathroom to shower. I'm left alone with my thoughts as I consider what she's offering me. I'm shocked, to be perfectly honest, that she is so willing to let me fuck Andrea. Even so, I'm also excited. Tonight will be a different experience for the both of us.

Chapter Nine: Intense Desires Awakened

58

We walk onto the yacht in the small harbor and soon the Dumonds greet us on the deck. "We're happy that you're here," Andrea says with a warm smile under the dim deck lights.

"Very happy," Simon adds as he reaches out and takes Renee's hand. He kisses it gently before reaching for and shaking mine. "So, was our talk worth it?"

I look at my wife. She still has considerable reservations about what might happen here tonight, but I'm very happy with the prospect of having sex with the beautiful Andrea Dumond.

"It was worth it, sure, but Renee isn't convinced," I tell him.

"I'm here for him more than for me," she tells them.

"Oh. I see." Andrea takes my wife by the hand. "Please follow us, gentlemen." The women disappear into the cabin of the large yacht. Simon and I follow, this time going downstairs into a large master bedroom that has a California king bed and beautiful porthole windows with sheer curtains. It's the sort of restful place that any ship owner would relish.

"Have a seat right here," Andrea says as she motions toward the bed. I do as she says and she has Renee sit down beside me. "I hope you both trust me." She smiles as she adds, "Oh, and pull off your clothes, Dominique."

"What?" My face heats up as I look at her standing in front of me.

"Just humor me, alright? I want to see you naked." Andrea's hands move over her body for a moment as she smiles at me. My cock begins to stiffen as I stand to my feet and do as she says. There is no way to hide my anticipation from my wife as I drop my shorts and briefs to the floor.

"Dom, you're hard," she whispers as she looks at my pecker.

"Renee, I'm sorry."

"No," Andrea says as she shakes her head. "No apologies." She then kneels to the floor and gets between my legs. "So, one of the things that has bothered you is that Renee has trouble swallowing, right?"

"Um, I guess so," I reply as her hands move over my thighs.

"Okay. Let's give you a little something that you need." Andrea slowly moves a hand to my pecker and then grips it lightly inside her hand before stroking it slowly.

"Oh, wow," I say as my body bucks a little.

Andrea looks over at my wife. "I like to give a guy a little tease with my hands to begin with. I never go straight to the oral stuff without prepping him a little." Her fingers move lightly over my piss hole and I feel some pre-come dribble out. Simon's wife then takes it and carefully rubs the natural lubricant all over the swollen red head of my cock.

"Very nice, dear," Simon says as he sits down nearby. He crosses a leg, likely to hide his own sexual excitement for what's going on.

"Do you like this?" Andrea asks as she plays with me.

"Yeah," I respond while grimacing. Her gentle touch is making me so horny as Renee watches us together. I wonder what my wife is thinking about as she watches what's going on right now?

"Good. I like to make men happy. Do you like to please your husband?" Andrea asks my wife.

Renee hesitates. "I guess that depends on what he wants in order to be pleased."

"Does that really matter?" she shakes her head. "Renee, you have to be ready to do whatever is necessary to make him happy. You expect the same from him, don't you?"

"He likes giving oral," my wife says to her. "It's not like I have to beg him."

"But, why does he like it so much?" Andrea tugs hard on my pole, causing quite a lot of pre-come juice to expel from the end of my dick. My body quakes as she moves the light lubricant over my shaft.

"I don't know. He must like the taste of me. I hate the taste of semen." Renee admits that she hates to have my spunk on her tongue. It bothers me to hear this again, though I already know as much.

"Semen flavor can change," Andrea tells her. "He might taste sweet or salty at times. Earthy or light. It depends on the man and what he eats." Simon's wife looks at me and says, "Here we go, Dominique." She bends down and kisses the tip of my cock before parting her lips and slowly sliding her mouth over my penis. The feeling is incredible as her lips tightly hug my phallus.

"Motherfucker," I grunt as she pushes the end of my manhood to the back of her throat. The sensation of her tongue moving around on the underside of my cock causes me to point my toes with pleasure.

"You're liking that, aren't you?" Renee asks as she looks over at me. "I can do that too."

"Fuck." I grip the edge of the bed as Andrea moves her mouth slowly up and down my cock. How do I answer my wife while another woman is giving me what could be the best blow job of my life?

Andrea slowly lifts her mouth from me and tells Renee, "Don't ever forget the balls." She pushes my cock back and takes in one of my balls, gently rolling it around inside her mouth as I pre-come onto my stomach.

"Shit, Andrea," I say as I breathe hard. I put one of my hands on the back of her head so that I can feel her soft, brown hair that is pulled back in a sexy ponytail. "Holy shit. Oh, fuck." The married woman then runs her tongue up the underside of my cock and pushes its girthy length all the way to the back of her throat again.

I begin to thrust lightly as I sit on the bed, my balls aching to release their contents now. "She's very good, huh?" Simon smiles as he watches his wife suck on my shaft. "She'll make you pop if she wants to. She can get you right to the edge and stop you, too."

"Fuck..." I feel myself begin to lose my seed. Instinctively, Andrea pulls her mouth off me and tightly grips the base of my cock, stopping me from ejaculating.

"Not yet," she tells me. Turning to my beautiful wife, she says, "Get into the floor with me, Renee." My wife looks at her with some apprehension, but soon she is on the floor with Andrea. "Hold on." Simon's wife goes back down on me and sucks slowly. I feel myself getting close to popping once again. Just as I begin to release, she stops me and pulls her mouth up. "Put your mouth on him, Renee. Get his penis as far back as you can. Remember, the goal is to have him come into your throat so that you don't have to taste his jism or get a sense of the texture. If he comes past your tonsils, you'll swallow automatically. It makes it easier."

"But..."

"Trust me." Andrea holds my cock hard as I want to come. My wife, though reluctant at first, opens her mouth and takes in my cock, pushing it to the back of her throat. "I'm going to make him come. When you feel it hit the back of your throat, just start swallowing." Andrea licks her finger and then pushes it into my asshole, causing me to jump a little. She finds my prostate and massages it hard as her other hand pulls on my balls.

"FUCK!!!" I suddenly spurt, my warm cum rocketing into the back of Renee's throat. She gags a little, but manages to swallow the first volley. *"FUCK!!! FFFFUUUUUCCKKKK!!!"* My orgasm is intense as Andrea continues to massage my balls and prostate. *"Uhhhh...fuck...ohhhh..."* I continue to come hard inside my wife's mouth without a drop of it coming out. Each time Renee swallows, the sensation causes more suction and a better feeling spurt. After about a dozen or so shots to the back of her throat, I begin to come off of my climax.

"That's good!" Andrea pulls her finger from my ass and watches as Renee sits up. "Did you swallow everything?"

My wife, obviously surprised, replies, "I think I did. Holy fuck, I *swallowed!*" Renee is excited as she looks at me. "You came in my mouth and I swallowed it! I didn't vomit, Dom!" She smiles at me as I nod my happiness.

"And so," Simon says to her. "What about the other thing?"

Renee's smile quickly disappears. "Anal? I can't do that. There isn't a special trick to stretching my asshole."

"You would be surprised." Simon stands to his feet and begins to remove his clothes. Andrea does too. It doesn't take them long to reveal their athletic attractive bodies. Simon's cock is longer than mine by a little, but not as girthy. His wife has nice round C-cup breasts and small, tight, dark nipples on them. I start to get hard again as I look at her body, including her trimmed twat. Though I thought I was completely spent moments ago, my cock begins to pre-come once again.

"Let me help you." Simon takes Renee's hand and helps her to her feet. He then carefully pulls up on her tee shirt before turning his attention to her bra, shorts and panties. "Waxed?" My wife nods her head. "Very nice." Simon lifts her up and sets her down on the bed before going down to eat her soft, wet pussy.

"Oh, fuck. You're good," Renee squeals as Simon's tongue moves around on her full labia. He finds her little lady bit and spends some time on it, eliciting more squeals and moans from her. I get hard and Andrea has noticed.

"Want to taste me?" she asks. I nod my head and Andrea gets up on the bed. She straddles my face and gently lowers her muff to me so that I can lap at her wet goodness. Her musky and sweet pussy juices are delightful as I eat her out.

"Simon," Renee whimpers. "You can fuck my pussy. Leave my asshole alone, though. Alright? Fuck my pussy, Simon." She doesn't want him to put his long snake inside her puckered back door. I get harder as I watch him press his cock against her wet pussy. Very slowly, he slides his bare shaft into my wife's wet hole.

"Baby," I say as I try to see my wife getting fucked. Andrea gets off me and lies back on the bed as she fingers herself and rubs her large clit. It grows and she pulls on it a little, causing more wetness to ooze from her sweet vagina.

"Fuck...oh, fuck."

"Does he feel good inside you, honey?" I ask my wife. She closes her eyes and just nods her head as he saws in and out of her pussy. Some of my pre-come drips onto the bed and I consider for a moment fucking Andrea hard. However, I don't want to miss any of this as my wife is fucked by another man.

Simon works on her for a while before pulling out his cock. "I want you on top, Renee. That way you can control everything better." They move around and he lays down on the bed. Renee lowers herself in reverse cowgirl position and her pussy swallows his cock. She moves around on top of him, grinding into his pecker hard as he enjoys putting his hands on her small breasts.

"This feels so good," Renee moans as his cock slides along her clit.

"It can feel better," Simon tells her. "Slide off of me and then lower your ass down."

"What?"

"Just trust me, Renee." My wife offers me a horrified look before doing this. She slowly puts her asshole against Simon's cock. He pulls on her a little and Renee winces. "It's okay. Just stay there for a moment," he tells her. I can tell that my wife would rather just get up and stop right now. However, she doesn't. Instead, she slowly lowers herself onto him and his cock soon disappears into her anus.

"It's all the way in," she says with surprise before rising and then dropping onto her lover. She continues this as she rubs her clit and I begin to rub my cock as I watch them together. "This is fucking intense," she says as her spinner body shakes.

"You're tight," he tells her as he helps my wife move up and down. Looking at me, Simon says, "You need to help her."

"What?"

"Get up and get between our legs." I do as he says and he pulls on Renee. "Lie back. You'll like this." Simon nods at me as I look down at my wife's blossoming pussy. He wants me to penetrate her this way as he fucks her in the asshole. I haven't done anything like this before, but I'm willing to see what it's like. I slide my cock into Renee's pussy and feel the other man's cock just on the other side of the thin walls that separate us. We both begin to thrust.

"Holy fuck. Oh, shit...too much," Renee tells us. "I'll tear."

"No you won't," Simon promises her. Andrea gets up and walks over to me. She reaches between my legs and plays with my balls as I fuck my wife with Simon.

"Dammit," I moan as I feel myself quickly getting primed to orgasm for a second time tonight.

"Ah..." Renee squeaks a little as she plays with her nipples. "Fuck. Holy fucking fuck..." Her pussy tightens around me as both Simon and I pump in and out of her holes, our ball sacks banging into each other.

"Uh..." Simon's eyes grow wide. "I'm close. Fuck. I'm going to come. *AHHHHH!!!*" I can feel his pecker pumping into Renee's ass through the wall of her vagina. *"Geez...FUCK!!!"* He seems a little surprised about the intensity of his orgasm as he releases into her. *"FUCK!!!"*

"NAHHHH!!!" Renee's small body trembles hard as she comes while sandwiched between us. *DOMINIQUE!!! FUCK!!! SIMON!!!"* She wriggles around between us and I begin to come inside her as well. Her tight pussy feels as if it's pulling my spunky soup into her womb.

"UHHHH!!! Ohhh...ohhh...ohhh..." I smack my balls hard into my wife as well as Simon. It's so strange to have sex with my wife at the same time someone else is fucking her, but I don't care while I come hard. *"Nahhhh...fuck...ohhhh..."* The experience is beyond anything I've had before, and I am certain I can say the same thing for Renee. She likes being pressed between two nakd men's bodies as she is fucked hard.

We begin to all finish our orgasms as Andrea sits down on the bed. I look at her and pull out of my wife. Pushing the other woman back, I shove my pussy soaked cock into her muff. *"HOLY FUCK!"* Simon's wife immediately shakes as she feels my cock strike her cervix. I'm so horny at this point that I'm worried I might actually pass out. It only takes a few strokes for Andrea to suddenly come. *"Ahhh...AHHHH!!!"* She bites her lower lip as she orgasms for me. *"Ahhhh..."* She grinds around on me and

I think that I might come again, but I don't. I'm spent but hard, so I'm able to at least help her to climax.

I pull out of Andrea and drop down to the floor at the side of the bed. "Shit. I can't believe I did that." My balls hurt badly as I shake my head. "I've never done anything like that before."

Simon smiles. "I think you might have made my wife a very happy woman."

"Very happy," she confirms between short breaths. "I didn't think that you would do that, Dominique."

"I wanted to," I tell her. Looking at Renee, I ask, "Was it good for you, baby?"

She nods her head while looking at the ceiling. "I think I like anal sex." We all laugh as semen drips from her pussy and asshole onto the bed. This little get-together tonight has changed my wife and I completely. I get the feeling that she will no longer complain about blow jobs and ass fucking now that we've actually done it with another couple. This is especially true since Renee has found that she enjoys anal sex.

Chapter Ten: A Different View

67

Renee and I snuggle close to each other as I wrap the beach blanket tightly around the two of us.

"They didn't say it would be so damned chilly this morning," my wife says to me as she shivers beside me. "Isn't it supposed to be warm in the Bahamas?"

I smile. "Well, it normally is. It seems that the storms that passed through just off the coastline brought along some cooler air with them. The temperatures are supposed to be back up later this afternoon, though." I kiss Renee's neck as I hold her close to me. My wife has and always will mean everything to me. The sex we had with the Dumond's the other night was great and it has opened up a lot of options for the two of us, but it's not what cements us together. It's our tenderness for each other that is key to our relationship.

"So, about Simon and Andrea," Renee says after some thought. "They really are very different people, aren't they?"

"Yeah, they are," I agree. "And I think we're a little different now, too."

"Well, sure, *now* we are," my wife giggles. "But it is because of them. I wonder how many other people are like them?"

I take a breath before kissing her neck again. Then I reply, "There have to be quite a few others, baby. I've been looking up swapping and partner sharing online and there are a lot of people who post their experiences there. I think we should probably do that too."

Renee turns her head to look at me. "Really? You want to tell others what happened between us and the Dumond's on their yacht?"

"Of course. We don't have to use our real names, though. We can change them so that you don't have to worry about people you know learning about our little secrets from Nassau." I smile at Renee and think about the sex that we had this morning before we came out here to greet the sunrise. She insisted on sucking me off and to completion and swallowing, which will never be something I get too used to. We haven't attempted anal sex again on our own just yet, but we have plenty of time to get to that. I'm happy with where we are right now.

"Would you ever do it again?" Renee asks. This surprises me a little. Yesterday she commented that what we did was a little too weird for her and that she probably wouldn't want to do that again with the Dumond's.

"I would like to," I admit. "And not just if you would like to. I myself would like to do that again with another couple. Would you?" I smile at Renee as my cock stiffens inside my shorts.

"I might," she replies. "Especially if the other couple is sweet and understanding. I feel like Andrea and Simon were very understanding, Dom. It made everything so much better for us."

"It did, didn't it?"

"Absolutely." Renee turns to look out over the water as she snuggles her back in against me. "Have you already been looking online?"

Chuckling, I reply, "You know that I have. And yes, I might have found a good couple in Ohio."

"Ohio? Really?" My wife seems very surprised. "And what do you want to do about this couple in Ohio?"

"I don't know. I guess I would like to message them and see about meeting in Columbus. That would make the most sense, right?"

She nods her head. "Yeah, it would. Go ahead and message them, then. Let's see what they have to say." I'm shocked to hear this from Renee. Just a few days ago, she was a woman who would have resisted any attempts at this sort of thing with me. She would have never allowed another woman to give me a blow job and she would have definitely not allowed another man to fuck her inside her ass. However, the Dumond's came along and changed all that for her. I'm thankful for that change. It means that our marriage will likely be that much better between us from now on.

"Come on, sun," I say as I look up at the overcast sky. The clouds have been thick this morning and unrelenting as the temperatures hover in the lower sixties. "Let's get this beach warmed up."

Renee giggles. "Maybe we should go back inside and make some more of our own heat, Dom. What do you think of that idea?"

I kiss my wife before answering, "I think that would be an awesome thing to do." We get up from the cool sand and begin our walk back to the hotel. If the sun won't give us heat here, we can make our own just as Renee has suggested. As a matter of fact, I look forward to enjoying her company in bed. Our marriage is much stronger now and our willingness to play with others has been reinforced. There's no doubt that we will enjoy our newfound sex life together. I look forward to sending a message to the other Ohio couple in the States when we get back home. It will be fun to further experiment with our newfound sexual freedoms by meeting other couples. It also wouldn't surprise me if Renee and I decided in the near future to come back and visit the Dumond's again. After all, we have them to thank for everything.

THE END

Don't miss out!

Visit the website below and you can sign up to receive emails whenever Karly Violet publishes a new book. There's no charge and no obligation.

https://books2read.com/r/B-A-GIXE-NDTQB

BOOKS 2 READ

Connecting independent readers to independent writers.

Did you love *Hotwife Vacation - A M F M Multiple Partner Wife Watching Wife Sharing Romance Novel*? Then you should read *Hotwife Hotel - A Hotwife Wife Sharing Open Relationship Romance Novel*[1] by Karly Violet!

[2]

A Hotwife, a hotel suite and a hot bartender - the perfect way to reignite the passion!

Heidi and Pierce have mutually agreed something needs to be done to reignite the passion in their dead bedroom. The married couple settle on a trip to Vegas to reintroduce the spark in their marriage. And when a strappng young bartender by the name of Gavin pays extra attention to the stunning wife Heidi...............Pierce decides to take the first step in bringing a handsome man into his beautiful wife's world!! *This 20,000*

---

1. https://books2read.com/u/38MlLV

2. https://books2read.com/u/38MlLV

About the Author

Sign up to my mailing list to receive the two free epilogues for 'A Hotwife Adventure' and 'Hotwife Training' and to stay up to date on all of my latest releases! http://eepurl.com/c3ICWf Sign up to my Patreon account and receive exclusive Hotwife stories every month and sexy scenes every week! https://www.patreon.com/karlyviolet

Read more at https://www.patreon.com/karlyviolet.

About the Publisher